For Amelia

First published 1995 by Walker Books Ltd
87 Vauxhall Walk, London SE11 5HJ

10 9 8 7 6 5 4 3 2 1

© 1995 Colin West

This book has been typeset in Plantin.

Printed in Hong Kong

British Library Cataloguing in Publication Data
A catalogue record for this book is
available from the British Library.

ISBN 0-7445-3766-5

One Day in the Jungle

COLIN WEST

WALKER BOOKS
AND SUBSIDIARIES
LONDON • BOSTON • SYDNEY

One day in the jungle
there was a little sneeze.

"Bless you, Butterfly!" said Lizard.

Next day in the jungle
there was a not-quite-so-little sneeze.

"Bless you, Lizard!" said Parrot.

Next day in the jungle
there was a medium-sized sneeze.

"Bless you, Parrot!" said Monkey.

Next day in the jungle
there was a big sneeze.

"Bless you, Monkey!"
said Tiger.

Next day in the jungle
there was a very big sneeze.

"Bless you, Tiger!"
said Hippo.

Next day in the jungle
there was an enormous sneeze.

"Bless you, Hippo!"
said Elephant.

Next day in the jungle
there was a **GIGANTIC** sneeze.

"Bless me!" said Elephant.
"I've blown away the jungle!"